The
PEREGRINE

The PEREGRINE

A Novel

Sue Picco

SUNSTONE
PRESS

SANTA FE

Sunstone books may be purchased for educational, business, or sales promotional use. For information please write: Special Markets Department, Sunstone Press, P.O. Box 2321, Santa Fe, New Mexico 87504-2321.

Book and Cover design ◆ Vicki Ahl
Body typeface ◆ WTC Our Bodoni
Printed on acid free paper

Library of Congress Cataloging-in-Publication Data

Picco, Sue, 1956-
   The peregrine : a novel / by Sue Picco.
      p. cm.
   ISBN 978-0-86534-800-4 (softcover : alk. paper)
 1. Fathers and sons--Fiction. 2. Soldiers--Fiction. 3. Grandfathers--Fiction.
4. Children of military personnel--Fiction. 5. Iraq War, 2003---Fiction.
6. New Mexico--Fiction. 7. Domestic fiction. I. Title.
   PS3616.I237P47 2011
   813'.6--dc22

                                    2010053845
le.

Published in

WWW.SUNSTONEPRESS.COM
SUNSTONE PRESS / POST OFFICE BOX 2321 / SANTA FE, NM 87504-2321 /USA
(505) 988-4418 / ORDERS ONLY (800) 243-5644 / FAX (505) 988-1025

To Roman and Max
and all those who stay behind

1

Kicked Out

What do I remember about last year? I was mad.

"Anger issues"—that's what the school counselor said. After I pounded Joey Cusumano's face in the playground sand, the principal of Holy Innocents Elementary school told my mother not to bring me back. I was the only fourth grader ever threatened to be permanently kicked out of school by Sister Rose of Lima.

Then the call came, and it didn't matter anyway. Dad's Humvee had been hit on the way to the Baghdad airport. He was in a hospital in Germany, and Mom wanted to be with him. She and my little sister, Bea, were going to Europe. "I have to take Bea with me; you know she's too young to go to Grandma and Grandpa's. I'm sorry, Ro, but you're the oldest, and I know you can make the trip by yourself." So now it was my turn to get shipped out. Mom was sending me to New Mexico where my grandparents lived.

"Just for a few months," she said, "until Dad is well enough to come home." I'd been there once. It was nice and all—for a visit. But Grandma and Grandpa lived five miles away from the nearest town and sixty miles away from a city with a movie theater!

I thought up all the reasons I could to tell Mom that I should stay in our house in Virginia.

"You could hire Jeannie to watch me at night," I pleaded. "I can take care of myself during the day."

"Right," she answered sarcastically. "Jeannie's in tenth grade, Ro. Her mom can't even leave *her* alone for more than a day."

Even though I hated school and most everybody in it, I still had a couple of friends I would miss. Besides, my dog Coyote. What would we do with him? I couldn't leave him behind. The phone rang but before she answered it, she knelt down, so we were at eye level, "I promise, Roman, this will only be for a little while. I need your help right now to keep this family together."

After badgering her for a week, hoping she'd change her mind about the whole move, Mom finally gave in a little bit—instead of sending Coyote to the kennel, she'd get him his own airplane ticket. "But you're still going to live with Grandma and Grandpa, and I want you to be polite and not just play with Coyote all day," she reminded me. When I made a face and kicked the table leg, she looked sternly, "You'll be surprised at what you'll find there."

2

Choices

The night before the trip, I thought about the last six months. How it had all started and why my family had ended up like this.

I'd been "acting out" for a while now, even before Dad's deployment. Sure, he'd worked overseas before. He'd even gone to fly fighter jets in Afghanistan, but it was only for two or three months at a time. He was *always* back in time for baseball season. When we lived in Alaska, he even had time to coach my T-ball team. That was the best. The other kids liked my dad. They even gave him a trophy at the end of the season, just for being a great coach. Now, I had a chance to be first string running back in football, and he'd never get to see a game.

Last summer, I'd heard them talking—loud voices, which my parents hardly ever used.

"If you have a choice," my mother challenged, "why do you want to do this? Why leave us for fifteen months?"

"Cindy," my dad started off nicely, "I've got to do this. I've got to fly more combat missions, so I can move us to a better place for our next assignment. Maybe move closer to my parents or yours," he pleaded, giving her logical reasons why he was leaving.

"You've already made up your mind, haven't you, Joseph? Talking to you is pointless," Mom's angry voice filled every corner of the kitchen.

"It's what we train for," Dad shot at back at her, like he was giving an order to one of his men.

"I know," she yelled. Then her voice got small, "I know, but I'm so afraid for you, and Joseph, the kids are so little." I could tell she had started to cry. My dad felt pretty bad about leaving us, but it didn't change his mind.

During the two weeks before he shipped out, Dad tried to spend as much time as he could with me, Mom and Bea.

"I'll call you as soon as I get to Kuwait," he said. But Mom told me that we might have to wait two or three weeks for that phone call and maybe, if he could find a computer, he'd be able to write a short e-mail once a week.

He asked me to help him pack for the trip, a father-son thing. I didn't want to help. Why should I? He chose to leave us; that's what he and Mom were fighting about. When the day came for his unit to go, he knew how I felt.

My dad led his unit in formation as they marched on the parade field. When he was done, he talked to us for one last time. "Be good to your mother and sister," he said to me. "I'm counting on you to help them." He just hugged my little sister and then kissed Mom. "Those fifteen months will be over soon, honey," he promised. All she could do was shake her head and say quietly, "I love you, Joseph."

We drove home from the base, Mom, me and Bea, in silence. I was mad, Mom was teary and trying not to show it, and Bea's usual three-year old chatter and singing was replaced by her just looking out the window into the rain.

3

The Lie

Football season had promised to be great, but turned out pretty lousy last year. I tried out for my YAFL team and made first string running back, just like I'd planned all summer. Then after Dad left something clicked, cracked, or got broken inside me.

I just didn't care anymore. I didn't care if I got the ball. I didn't care if I kept my first string spot. I didn't even care if I played anymore.

It was more fun to mess around at practice than do what Coach wanted. After the first few practices, he could tell that I hadn't memorized the plays. Heck, he could tell that I hadn't even opened the play book! I didn't know any of the game plans, and I'd made up my mind that I wasn't going to learn them.

"What's the matter, Rodriguez?" he asked, walking me to the sidelines.

I just shrugged up my shoulders, "I dunno..." But I didn't finish the rest of the sentence that was floating to the front of my brain, "and I don't care."

It would have been easier for all of us, if I had just said "I quit" that day. The next week I went to practice late, and I was punished with a couple of extra laps.

"Fine," I told Coach sarcastically, "I like to run." He just shook his head.

After that, I started forgetting equipment, so I couldn't practice. I'd show up without my mouthpiece, forget my helmet, or have on my tennis shoes instead of cleats. I'd do warm-ups, then sit on the side-lines, pull at the grass and talk to a few of my friends when they came off the line.

Then one day, I went to practice without my shoulder pads and Coach told me, "Listen, Rodriguez, I can see you're not interested this year. Why don't you just go home? Think about whether you want to be in football. Then come back for tryouts next fall."

He didn't say it mean, just like a fact. And I knew he was right. I should have been hurt and upset by losing my spot on the team, but honestly, I just didn't care. What was the point of showing up every day just to sit on the sidelines?

Mom worked each day from noon to 5:30 at Bea's pre-school. She'd never know that I wasn't in football anymore. I figured I'd just let her keep thinking I was going to practice. I wouldn't tell her until I had to. So every day, I went home, got a snack, played video games and went outside to play with Coyote.

Each night I made sure my muddy cleats were by the back door with my helmet and shoulder pads, so she could see that I'd used them. As she cooked dinner, Mom would ask me the usual, "How was school? How was practice?"

"Okay," I'd mumble.

"Well, tell me about it," she'd smile and turn back to the stove.

"I gotta go wash my uniform," I'd tell her, stalling my answer. For two weeks, I threw my perfectly clean uniform in the washer every day.

When the first game day arrived, Mom was all set. She was wearing blue and gold, my team's colors, and bounced into my room early. That memory hurt.

"Big game today, Rome. I've got a good breakfast for you downstairs. But I want you to have enough time to eat and digest in case you get tackled," she winked, remembering how I'd "lost" my breakfast last year when I ate right before the game.

I got up and dressed in my football uniform. We bundled up Bea and drove to the game. Mom was chattering away at me, but I felt like I was in a fog. Pre-game warm ups were just about ready to start when we drove up. As we got out, Coach gave Mom a puzzled look then quickly walked over.

"I'm sorry Mrs. Rodriguez, but Roman isn't playing today."

"What?" she asked. "Why, did he do something?" She questioned Coach, still not understanding. I stood off to the side.

"Ma'am, your son hasn't come to practice for over two weeks now," Coach said, gently. "He didn't tell you?"

She looked down at me, mad and hurt. Then put on her adult face, "Well, thanks for everything you've done for him, Coach. We won't be staying for the game. I hope the Tigers have a great season." She smiled, but only with her lips; her eyes looked real sad.

"Sure," Coach put his hand on my mom's shoulder and lowered his voice. "I'm sorry it has to be this way. Maybe he just misses Joseph..."

But before he could finish, Mom grabbed my shoulder and pushed me to the car.

It would have been better if she had just yelled at

me, but she calmly told me to get in the back. She buckled Bea into her car seat, then got in to the driver's side, put her forehead against the steering wheel and started to cry. "What is wrong with you, Roman? I need you to be better than this," she said, not looking at me.

Sure, I felt bad, really bad for her, but I wasn't budging. I was mad, and I was going to stay that way. When we got home, she didn't have to tell me to go to my room. I didn't feel like being around people anyway, especially not my family.

Later, I came downstairs for a snack, hoping I could sneak by her.

"Roman, I just have one question for you," she cornered me by the refrigerator. "What were you doing all the time you were supposed to be at practice?" She looked kind of scared and worried, so I told her the truth.

"I just came home and played video games, or took Coyote outside and tossed the ball to him."

"Are you sure?"

That made me mad. "Yeah. Don't you believe me?"

"Why should I, Roman? You've lied to me for several weeks," she turned away. "Your father and I expect much better behavior and honesty from you."

"Yeah, and I expected him to be here for me— especially this year, when I was first string," I spat the words out, angry at her, my dad and myself.

We stood, staring at each other across the kitchen until she yelled, "Just go to your room and stay there until dinner-time. You're on restriction for the rest of the month."

4

Hollow Days

Halloween, Thanksgiving and Christmas went by with Mom trying to make the holidays as normal as possible. But it didn't really work. We went to the base for Thanksgiving dinner. "Who wants to cook a turkey for three?" I heard her tell a friend over the phone. "Besides, Joseph always helped with dinner, and I'm just not up to it this year."

Christmas was okay. I helped put the lights on the tree since that was always Dad's job. I opened a couple of presents from Mom then put the rest aside. It didn't really matter what I got anyway. Bea was still excited, but there was no one for her to jump on and wake up on Christmas morning except me. Mom was already up, drinking a lonely cup of coffee on Christmas morning and waiting for the phone to ring. Dad called in the afternoon, about three in the morning Baghdad time. It was really good to hear his voice.

"Hey, Christmas is already over on this side of the ocean," he told me. "But I guess you guys just opened up what Santa brought a few hours ago. Did you like the stuff he gave you?" I made sure he knew how much Bea liked her presents.

"Be careful, Dad," I said at the end of our conversation.

"You too, Buddy. Don't worry about me though; this base is just like a country club. They've got a Pizza Hut and Taco Bell within walking distance." We laughed about the restaurants and how we liked the greasy fast food that mom usually didn't let us have.

"Okay, Son, let me talk to your mom," he said. She carried the phone into the bedroom.

"Well, hearing your father in such good spirits has put me in a much better mood," she stated, smiling. "Your dad is having pizza for supper. How 'bout if we get pizza delivered, and I make popcorn?"

"Yay," Bea was thrilled. Before Mom was done in the kitchen, we put a blanket on the floor and flipped on the TV. With the tree lights on, the phone call from Dad and some junk food, we were actually able to find some holiday spirit watching reruns of *A Christmas Story* on cable.

School started in January and we were all pretty relieved to get back into the routine. I was doing better in spelling, but Joey Cusumano sat right behind me. Every time we passed our tests back to check them, he'd always mess up my score. Whenever that happened, I'd trip him on the way to recess; it ended in a bloody lip for Joey, and a trip to the principal and a two-day suspension for me. Our teacher, Sister Peter Ann wanted us to settle the issue and told us we had a special project—to work out a plan so we could get along together. She wanted it by Friday, February 13, "and it will count for a grade," she said, raising her eyebrows as a warning. Just my luck, I guess.

I showed Sister my plan, which I refused to work on with Joey, and he showed her his plan.

"Seems like you both think you should do the same things," she said in our after school meeting.

"Joey, you stop marking Roman's tests incorrectly and Roman, you stop tripping him," she pointed at Joey. "And no more fighting. Agreed?"

"Yeah, okay," we both mumbled.

"Good, shake hands and don't come out swinging," she laughed at her own joke, then said, "This better work boys or I'm going to have another talk with your parents. Now, go home and have a good weekend."

The next day was Valentine's Day. Mom was surprised when the florist's truck pulled up with a huge box for her. Dad had ordered a dozen red roses for her all the way from Iraq. Her whole face was smiling, and I hadn't seen that for a while. She was putting them in a vase when she heard another knock.

"Who could that be?" she asked happily, and nearly skipped to the door. From the kitchen I heard her slowly repeat the word "No." She began low and soft but got louder with every breath. "No, no, no, no!" I ran into the entry way. The Air Force chaplain was helping her into the front room, helping her sit down.

"He's injured," the officer continued. "It's bad, but he'll make it." Another officer took my little sister to the kitchen to get her some milk and cookies. She was too young to understand why Mom was shaking and crying and nearly hysterical, but I listened on the other side of the living room doorway as the chaplain explained about Dad and the explosion.

"His vehicle was hit pretty hard, but they were able to get him out and get medical attention within minutes of the bombing," the chaplain continued. "He's in stable condition at Ramstein Air Base in Germany, Mrs. Rodriguez, but he hasn't woken up yet. If you can get out there, the Air Force can put you up on base."

"Yes, yes, I'll have to think," Mom said, quietly. "Of course, I'm going, but I need to think about the children."

As the officers walked toward the door together, they both said how badly they felt. Mom thanked them, closed the door, then walked into the kitchen to smell the roses Dad had sent.

5

Going Solo

So at the end of February, Mom, Bea and I headed to the airport. They were going east to Europe and Ramstein. Coyote and I flew west to Albuquerque. The flight attendant made sure we got on the right train to Santa Fe where my dad's friend met Coyote and me.

Lorenzo was my dad's best friend in high school. When Dad left for college at the Air Force Academy in Colorado Springs, 'Renzo stayed close to home to take care of his uncle's farm.

He'd come to visit Dad and us wherever we moved. When Dad got stationed in Alaska, 'Renzo brought us red chile "from home," so he and my dad could make tamales for Christmas. That was the best Christmas dinner ever! I remembered that it was dark and cold all day long, the arctic night, but our family was all together and happy. That was the year, 'Renzo brought Coyote for my present. "Every boy needs a dog," he told my mom, and Dad couldn't say no to his best friend.

I saw him as soon as I got off the train at the Santa Fe station. "Hey, Buddy," he gave me a special handshake we had worked out on his last visit. "Let's go get Coyote out of the baggage compartment and give him a chance to stretch his legs." We found Coyote, clipped the leash on him and let him out. Then 'Renzo put the cage in the back of his truck.

As we walked, he told me how big I'd grown and how Coyote was looking good. I knew he wanted it to be nice and friendly between us, but I remembered I was still angry about this trip. Besides, I was tired, and I didn't feel like talking. I'd already been in a car, on a plane, then a train, and I would have to take a bus pretty soon to a place I didn't want to go. I was entitled to be mad. So every time he asked me a question, I just said, "Yes, No, or Okay." He got the message, but tried to coax me out of my mad mood.

"Since you're so talkative, let's shut you up with some food," he chuckled, and we headed to a little hamburger place where Coyote and I could sit outside in the winter sunshine.

"Two Lotta combos," he ordered at the outside window, "and two chocolate shakes." Well, he'd remembered that I liked chocolate. I knew he was trying. When we sat down to eat, he asked some questions about me, Mom and the trip. He mentioned again how grown up Coyote was. He was running out of stuff to say, and I was only interested in my own thoughts about Mom and Bea traveling alone all the way to Europe.

Then he asked the question I'd been answering for the last couple of weeks. "You worried about your dad?" He looked at me, with a question in his eyes, hoping I'd say no, so we could talk about football or something.

"Yeah." I gave him my "duh" look in return. Of course, I was worried. My whole family was messed up because of the war. Dad was always gone, and I wasn't sure if I'd ever see him again. "I hate this stupid war," I said, looking down at my half eaten burger.

"Me too, Ro," he said quietly, then sniffed and blinked.

That question about Dad had the same effect on every adult who asked me. They thought I was going to be the one to break down crying. They seemed surprised that they couldn't handle it as well as a nine year old kid. They'd probably have liked it if I cracked, but Mom had cried enough for all of us since the Air Force told her about Dad. She tried to hide it, but I figured sometimes if a person starts to cry over a thing this serious, they might not be able to stop when they need to.

"Mind if I give Coyote the rest of this?" I asked, not looking at 'Renzo. "I'm not really hungry."

"Nah, man, that's okay. Wait here a minute. I'll go get him some water."

Coyote sat obediently waiting for me to say it was okay to eat. That was one of Dad's rules—no begging at the table. "I don't care how much he cries," Dad would say, "you have to be tough enough to make him obey." Coyote separated the meat from the bun and gobbled up the hamburger, leaving the onions, lettuce and tomatoes on the concrete. I fed him the few fries I had left, one by one, dipped in ketchup and mustard, just the way he liked them.

I started to feel bad for 'Renzo when he came out with the water. He looked so down. I seemed to be doing that a lot lately, making people really mad or sad and making them worry about me. I knew I didn't have to be such a jerk, but... "Hey, 'Renzo," I flashed him a smile, "thanks for lunch. It really was good. And I'm glad we came to a place where Coyote could eat too."

He laughed and ruffled up my hair. Looking at his

watch, I figured it was time to go, "Well, I better take you and your world traveling wonder dog to the bus station."

When we got to the truck, Coyote cried about going in his carrier. "Sorry, but I already had to bribe the bus driver to take you all the way to El Puerto. I don't think he'll let Coyote on without his cage." We drove to the station a few blocks away.

'Renzo walked me to the bus. "Hey, Eugenio," he told the driver, "take care of my friend and his dog."

"Sure, where they going?" asked Eugene.

"El Puerto. This is Junior's boy."

"El Puerto. That's the end of the line for this old New Mexi Bus," he joked. "Welcome aboard, Junior's boy."

"It's Roman," I corrected.

"Sure, Boss. Let's get that luggage stowed." As he went back to take care of Coyote's cage and my suitcase, 'Renzo told me, "Don't worry Ro, you'll be okay." Then he knelt down and told me, "I'm praying for your dad." I nodded and jumped on the bus before 'Renzo could give me a goofy handshake good-bye.

I could see him waving at me, hoping I'd wave back, until the bus turned the corner to go out of town.

6

El Puerto

It was late when the New Mexi Bus made its last stop—the church plaza at El Puerto. After a turn off from the highway and a few twists and turns down narrow streets, Eugenio pulled to a stop.

"Hey, Junior's Boy, we're here. The hot spot of the desert southwest," he chuckled, "El Puerto, New Mexico."

"What?" I was groggy from the long nap. When I looked around, I was the only passenger on the bus, and it was already starting to get dark.

"Look, there's your grandpa," Eugenio announced and climbed down to get Coyote's carrier. I grabbed my backpack.

Grandpa gave the driver a five dollar bill with his thanks for bringing me so far. "It wasn't nothing, Mr. Rodriguez. Besides that," he laughed, "I got paid on the front end by Lorenzo. If you gotta put that five dollars somwheres, just stick it in the collection plate at church for me. I need all the help I can get." He patted Grandpa Joe on the back, then climbed up the bus stairs, revved up the engine and was gone, a narrow cloud of dust trailing behind him.

Grandpa Joe was glad to see me and gave me a big

hug. "How you been, boy?" He smiled and smelled like tobacco and wind.

"I'm okay, Grandpa." I tried to smile, but my face was kind of frozen from standing in the cold. I had forgotten about the high country, the mountains and how cold it could get here. Dad told me that it sometimes snowed on the highest peaks in May, and I could see the outline of those mountains, snow capped and turning pink in the setting sun.

He bent down and looked in at Coyote in his dog carrier. "Does this guy need to take a walk before we load him into the truck?" I was going to say that Coyote could ride in the truck's cab with me, but before I did, Grandpa had him out of the cage and was letting him run around the small village plaza.

I was worried. "Hey, he doesn't know what to do if he's not on his leash," I yelled. "Here, Coyote, here boy!" He was busy sniffing up the whole place, and he pretended like he couldn't hear me at all. Then Grandpa gave one sharp whistle, and Coyote came running over.

"That's the way you call a dog, Roman," he said. He used the Spanish pronunciation of my name, with the accent on the last syllable. Mostly the kids at school in Virginia just called me Ro because they couldn't really say my name right. Grandpa pronounced it the way my dad said it when he was mad, or my mom did when she was serious. But when I looked at him, Grandpa Joe was smiling and opening the tailgate on the truck. He put my suitcase and Coyote's carrier in the back. Then Coyote jumped in.

"Grandpa, Coyote can ride up front with me," I tried to convince him, worried about losing my best friend on the first night in El Puerto. "He might fall out of the truck or even jump out when we're moving."

Grandpa looked at me and laughed, "Not if he knows what's good for him." The old red Ford truck bumped the entire five miles to "the *rancho*", and I watched Coyote through the rear window the whole way. He sucked in the cold air and let his cheeks puff out. His tail wagged the entire trip to Grandpa Joe's, and he only fell over once, when we took a big bump at the cattle guard. Still, I didn't like him riding back there—too many bad things could happen to him.

Grandma was waiting on the front porch when we got to the house. Of course, she had a broom in her hand. That was how I remembered her from my one visit, either cleaning or cooking. Not like my mom. She had to do a million things all at the same time, especially when Dad was away, and she always seemed to be on the road in the minivan.

"*Hito*," she smiled as I got out of the truck. Then came the big hug, and I was wrapped up in three layers of her sweaters and woolen gloves for about a minute or two. Grandpa was unloading my stuff, and Coyote had already jumped out of the truck and was sniffing around the chicken coop.

"It's freezing out here, Maria. The boy is cold; stop all this hugging and let's feed this poor guy," Grandpa winked at me. And Grandma laughed. As we walked into the house, I questioned, "Will Coyote be..."

"Yeah, he'll be fine," Grandpa told me. "Unless he eats one of my chickens. Then you and I will have a talk with him." He got a mean look on his face, kind of like Dad. I didn't think he would be mean to Coyote, but I didn't know for sure.

Inside the house, it smelled kind of good and kind of old. The good part was the wood in the fireplace and the stove. It smelled sort of fresh, like the outside had been brought inside. There was a stack of small logs by the cooking stove. "Be careful of that stove, Roman," Grandma said, "It's not like the kind you have in the city. It's hot all the way around." I'd never seen anything like it except in the books I read about American history, like Abe Lincoln's cabin.

"Do you guys have electricity?" I was worried because I wanted to make sure I could plug in my cell phone, so I could talk to Mom.

Both of them started laughing. "Sure we do," said Grandpa. He winked at Grandma, "We even got electric lights and everything." He flicked the switch a couple of times to make his point.

"Don't pay attention to him, Roman," she bantered. "He's pulling your leg. I just prefer cooking on my wood stove, like my grandmother did. In fact, this is her old stove."

"Wow," I said and asked, "was it like this when my dad lived here?"

"Yes," she answered, "including my extra special *bizcochitos*." She brought out a plate of cookies, and that was the second best smell. Cinnamon, sugar and anise, like licorice, filled the air.

After my fifth cookie and two glasses of milk, I asked, "Why do these taste so good, Grandma? My mom never makes cookies like this."

She smiled and pointed toward the stove. "Sometimes, Roman, the old ways are the best ways."

Well, that first night in El Puerto was good. Even after all the traveling, I found out that I might like it here at the *rancho*. Coyote was waiting for me on the porch when I went to find him. He looked happy, too.

Since it was Thursday, they wouldn't take me to school until Monday, but Grandma reminded me that bedtime was soon, and I'd better get ready. By the time I got done in the bathroom, they had already brought Coyote inside.

"Too cold for him out there tonight," Grandpa said. "He's going to bunk in your room tonight, Roman, if that's okay with you." He winked.

"Yeah, sure, that's great." Wow, I thought, Mom would never let Coyote sleep in the same room with me. Now he could sleep on the bed. As Grandpa walked upstairs, he warned me quietly, "Don't say anything about Coyote in your room tonight. We'll let Grandma know tomorrow how he didn't chew on her quilt and didn't mess up her rug. Right?"

"Sure, Grandpa Joe." Now it was my turn to wink.

7

The *Rancho*

My room was actually my dad's old room. It was cool to see the things that he played with as a kid. All his model airplanes were still on the shelves, and some hung from fishing line from the ceiling. He had been in love with flying ever since he was a little boy. I wondered why, especially here. Maybe he just wanted to go off and be something different, not a farmer or a rancher, but something else that was dangerous and exciting.

But, it didn't seem fair that Dad had been gone so long from home, and now he was hurt. I didn't want a job like his. I liked the fact that Grandpa Joe and Grandma stayed at home; everything was settled here, and people seemed to stay in the same place for a while. I went to sleep that night, Coyote at the foot of my bed.

Morning came early the next day.

"Roman," Grandma whispered in my ear as she sat on the edge of my bed. "It's time to get up."

I sat up in the still dark morning. She was clucking over the fact that Coyote was on the bed but only said, "*Ay, Joe!*" in exasperation.

"Come on, Roman, there's work to do."

"Work," I mumbled groggily and rubbed the sleep out of my eyes. "It's still night out."

"Not on the farm. Come down and get your breakfast, and then Grandpa Joe has some things for you to do." She kissed my forehead and called Coyote to come with her.

Okay, okay, I thought, I'm coming. But what kind of work did they do in the middle of the night? Even on a farm, you have to see where you are going. I pulled on my jeans and t-shirt. It was cold in my room. I listened for the heater to come on, like it did at home. Nothing... I found my jacket and wondered what kind of a house this was where you had to wear your coat to breakfast!

Downstairs, I could hear Grandma cooking and Grandpa Joe sitting down to his first cup of coffee. "Hey, Sleepy," he called out when he saw me. "Were you gonna stay in bed all day?"

Grandma cautioned him, "Joe, let him alone. They don't get up this early in the city."

"Gotta learn how to catch that early worm," Grandpa Joe grinned. I guess he was always kidding around, but I didn't feel like laughing this early. It was a lot warmer in the kitchen, so I didn't need my coat. I warmed my hands on the hot cup of cocoa Grandma had set at my place.

"Here, Roman," Grandma put a plate of bacon and eggs in front of me with a slice of homemade bread.

"Do you have any Fruity Loopers?" I asked. That's what I had every day at home.

"Not today," she patted my head. "Eat up because you'll need your energy. Grandpa's going to show you the land today."

I tried a bite. It was good, not Fruity Loopers, but it

was good. I guess it was so early, I forgot to say thanks for breakfast, but Grandma could tell how much I liked it since I ate everything.

The sun just started to peek through the trees when Grandpa told me it was time to go. "Let's take Coyote," he said as we headed toward the truck. "He'll need to know the way home in case he ever gets lost."

"That's what I'm afraid of," I mumbled under my breath.

I was real quiet in the truck. Tired and mad again. I didn't like getting up this early, and even though Grandma was nice to me and breakfast had been pretty good, I really didn't want to be here, without my mom and Bea. And Grandpa, with all his joking around... I knew this was going to be a long day.

In fact, I wondered what Mom and Bea were doing right now. I had my cell phone with me and tried to call, but there was no service yet. They were probably still flying to Germany. I thought of all the things that could go wrong. What if they missed their flight? What if Bea got lost? She had a habit of wandering away without telling us. What if the plane crashed? I scared myself so much with that one that I had to stop thinking for a while.

I put my face in my hands, trying to get rid of these crazy thoughts about my family. Grandpa jumped in the truck and saw me; I guess he thought I was just tired because he gunned the engine and said, "Wake up, Roman. It's a beautiful world out there." I looked up. Coyote was in the back of the truck, looking happy and excited. We were ready to roll.

8

We Save Beans

The part of the drive that stunk was the gates; the first couple were pretty easy to open but there must have been a hundred of them on the ranch. It was cold that day and felt even colder when I'd get out of the warm truck, open the gate, then wait for Grandpa to drive the truck through and close it.

"Geez, Grandpa," I complained, "how many more gates are there?" I kept thinking that they should just have solar collectors on the gate posts and hook them up, so the gates could open from a remote control inside the truck. "Ever think about solar power?" I mumbled, but Grandpa Joe heard me.

"*Ay*, Roman, just like your dad. Always trying to improve things around here. Which is good, don't get me wrong. But of what use would a grandson be if he couldn't help his *abuelo* open the ranch gates? You're too little to do much else." He knocked me on the head with his fist. Dad did that too when we were playing around, but I started thinking about why he left the ranch in the first place. Maybe this was one of the reasons.

We rode along in silence until it started to snow; a few flakes coming down. It was peaceful here and big. The landscape was huge, dotted with little hills and dark mesas spread across the horizons. Grandpa Joe stopped the truck for a minute and turned to me, "Most of this land is ours or belongs to our family." He looked at me and smiled. "Roman, you look just like your dad sitting there, pouting because you had to open a few gates," he said. I was sort of shocked by the way he knew me already, but I guess he had practice with my dad.

"I'm not pouting," I tried to defend myself then smiled because even I knew that he could see right through me.

"I miss them," was all Grandpa Joe needed to say as he put his foot on the gas and kept his eyes straight ahead on the dirt road.

"Me too."

We drove up to a little area where Grandpa had a goat herd of about ten females or does. Each year they all had babies about this time, so he said we needed to check them out and put bands on their ears to identify them in case they wandered into the neighbor's pastures.

Grandpa didn't raise cattle anymore. "Too old and tired to climb on a horse every day," he laughed. "When your dad lived here, he was in the saddle all day long in the summer. He was one of my best cowhands, and he knew exactly how to throw a calf down and brand him just right."

Suddenly, the truck jammed to a stop. Grandpa was out of the truck waving his hands and yelling like a crazy person. Then I saw it. A coyote, a real one, was dragging a goat away. The goat hung limply in the coyote's mouth as he ran toward the hills. Grandpa chased him as far as the fence. It had really started snowing, so I lost sight of him for a minute.

I'll admit it; I was too scared to get out of the truck. It was just me and Grandpa Joe out there, and what if he got attacked. My own Coyote was barking like crazy. I got out and ordered him to "stay" in the back of the pick-up. Then I saw Grandpa come back to the herd and bend down. He waved to me to come over. I heard him yell, "Roman, there's a blanket behind the seat. Bring it over here. I need it." He already had his warm winter coat off and had put it around something.

"Here, Grandpa," I ran with the blanket and looked down to see blood in the snow. Then I heard a strange sound, kind of like when Bea is playing with her dolls, and one of them is crying. Inside Grandpa's coat was a little goat baby.

"Here, let's wrap her up." Grandpa exchanged his coat for the blanket, and we carried the crying goat kid to the truck. "She's cold," Grandpa was breathing hard. "Let's get her inside to warm up."

"I can carry her, Grandpa," I volunteered. And even though she was heavy, I knew I could stop her crying once we got inside the warm truck. Somehow, I don't even remember opening gates on the way back. I was just concerned with the little goat. She was still shivering, so Grandpa told me to rub her all over to get her blood flowing. She nuzzled my hand and started sucking on my fingers.

"She's hungry," Grandpa smiled. "Glad we got to her before she became coyote food."

"What will you do with her, now that she doesn't have a mother?" I asked. "Will another goat become her mom?"

"No, probably not. She's the first born of the season, so the other goats don't have anything to feed her yet."

I was so worried about her. She was an orphan now.

I grabbed her from the middle of the seat where she was laying and held her in my arms for the rest of the ride home. Her gold, goat eyes looked at me, and she snuggled up against my chest until she fell asleep. I talked to her and told her not to worry.

In a way, we were both orphans. I had always been afraid of that—what if my dad got killed in the war and something happened to my mom? That thought was always lurking in my head, and sometimes it made me crazy thinking about it.

By the time we were back home, it was afternoon. I had dozed off in the warm truck. Grandpa woke me up, and I carried the baby goat inside.

"You're back early," said Grandma.

"We brought you a present, *Jefa*," Grandpa said with a big smile. He always called her *Jefa* which means, The Boss Lady, when he had something special to ask her.

"Look Grandma," I showed her just enough of the little goat's head so she could see. "Can we keep her?"

"Oh, Joe, what happened?" she asked anxiously.

"Let the young one tell you; he saw it all," said Grandpa Joe. "I need a good cup of coffee."

As I told the whole story, I could see how impressed Grandma and Grandpa were that I had seen the whole thing and had run to help. "And now Grandma, we need to figure out how to get her a new mother," I ended. She bent down and kissed me.

"Thank God the boy was with you," she scolded Grandpa Joe. "You are too old to be running around after coyotes."

Then Grandma shone her big eyes on me and knelt

down to see the *cabrito*. "Oh, she's beautiful—just a baby. I think I know a person who could become her mother," she winked at Grandpa Joe, but I didn't know what she was talking about.

"Up there, in the top cabinets, Joe. Get down the nipples and the bottle." Grandma started issuing orders. The goat was waking up and calling for her mother.

"Roman, you hold her and don't let her get away." Grandma ran to the pantry to get some canned milk and warmed it on the stove. When she gave me the bottle, I wasn't sure what to do, but Grandma guided my hand.

"Tip the bottle up like this. See, she likes it." She patted my shoulder and kissed me on the head. "You will make a great mother!"

9

School Bells

All weekend long, I took care of my baby goat. I named her Beans because she had little spots all over her and because that name sort of reminded me of my sister, Bea. At night, Beans would sleep in the kitchen and during the day, she would run around on the screened porch. But mostly, she and I and Coyote would play together in the yard.

I was having a surprisingly good dream about Beans early Monday morning. I saw her running around the pasture with the other goats. She stopped to talk to me and offered me a mouthful of grass. "Try it," she said in my dream, then ran off, her goat bell tinkling. Well, actually it sounded kind of like the phone downstairs, which woke me up. I looked at the clock—2:17 and still dark, and I fell back to sleep.

When Grandma came to wake me, she said cheerfully, "Time for school." Then sat on my bed and stroked my hair, "You look so much like your father," a pause, then, "Oh by the way, your mom called from Germany."

That news got me wide awake. I sat right up in bed and started asking questions. "Are they okay? How's Dad? How come you didn't let me talk to them?"

"Slow down," she smiled. "The call came about two

fifteen this morning, but your mom will call again soon to talk to you. Their trip was good, but Bea is exhausted, and your dad is doing fine."

Fine. What did she mean by that? "When can I talk to him?" I asked.

"In a little while," she hedged. I could tell she didn't really know the answer.

"But not next time. It will just be your mom and Bea." Grandma stopped and looked down at me, "She misses you."

I laid back down and put my head under the pillow.

"Hey, mister," she reminded me, tapping the pillow, "Breakfast in fifteen minutes—don't be late."

"Okay," I gave a muffled reply. I wondered what Mom and Dad and Bea were doing right now. I hardly ever wanted to talk to Mom and Bea before, now I needed to talk to them.

Going to school wasn't going to be much fun. I knew it. Kids can be mean, especially when you go to a new school in the middle of the year. Nobody knows your name, and they always make the goodie-two-shoes kid take you around for a day or two. In this family, Grandpa said that education was a good thing, but that Grandma was the person who dealt with the schools.

So after breakfast, even though I begged her to let me stay home one more day, Grandma drove us into town to register and get to class.

"What about Beans? Who's gonna take care of her, Grandma?" I asked as she started up the truck.

"Beans will be fine," she smiled. "I'll give her a bottle this morning and let her play in the yard. She'll be ready to eat again when you come home."

"Okay," I muttered softly, pouted and looked out the window.

"Are you worried about school?"

"No, not really," I tried to sound confident, but what if the kids were mean or even worse, what if they didn't talk to me at all.

"You know that you'll be in the same grade as Frankie Maestas."

"So...," I was trying to be snotty, so she'd just take me home, and I could play with Beans.

"*Ay,* Roman," she sounded exasperated. "So, he's a second cousin, and he'll take care of you today. That is if you don't act like a stubborn *cabrito* just eating trash and spitting it back out at people who are trying to help you."

"Hey," I said, looking surprised at Grandma, "I know what that means, and I'm not going to be a little goat." Grandma kept her eyes on the road. I figured I had hurt her feelings. I sometimes do that, especially when I'm scared or nervous.

"Sorry, Grandma."

"Okay, *mi hito,* but let me tell you that these are our friends, neighbors and relatives in this valley. We already love you because you belong to us. You don't have to prove anything to be loved here in El Puerto."

I stayed silent, thinking. Nobody had ever said anything like that to me before. With Dad in the Air Force, I'd already been in three schools. I started kindergarten in Maine and gone to second and half of third in Alaska. At my last school, I had to take on Johnny Cusumano's gang the first day. I guess I never really got that out of my head; Dad says you should forgive, but don't ever forget when somebody crosses you. I didn't forgive, or forget—except one thing, Dad's other rule; never throw the first punch. That's what got me suspended at Holy Innocents.

Grandma and I walked in just as the first bell was ringing. The front office was warm and friendly and painted the bright yellow of the New Mexico flag. In red, across the top of the wall read: Welcome to Zia Elementary. Home of the Roadrunners.

"Hey, Maria," said the smiling secretary behind the front office desk, "How are you? Is this Junior's boy?"

Junior. That's what they used to call Dad here. I wondered why he and mom didn't name me Joseph; now I knew. He probably wished he had a first name of his own.

"Yes, he's ready for his first day." Grandma reached down and put her hand on my shoulder. "Roman, this is Mrs. Martinez. She's the school secretary. If you need me for anything just tell your teacher or Mrs. Martinez, and they'll help you."

"That's right, Roman. I went to school with your dad, right here in this very building. In fact, he was in Mrs. Sanchez fourth grade class, too."

I guess Grandma was right. It seemed like everybody knew me already. Since everybody knew my dad, it was kind of like having a big brother who paved the way for me to be here. We filled out some paperwork, then Mrs. Martinez took Grandma and me to my new classroom. They walked behind me, and I could hear them talking in low voices between the clicks of Mrs. Martinez' heels on the wood floor.

"So, have you heard how he is?" Mrs. Martinez sounded concerned.

"*Por Dios*, not really. Cindy called us from Germany

early this morning, but he's still in intensive care," Grandma said, crying the last little bit. She took a tissue out of her purse and blew her nose.

"Right here, Roman," Mrs. Martinez called out. "Room four." I heard her tell my grandma that she would pray for Dad and light a candle for him at the church. Then she knocked on the door, gently pushed me inside and handed Mrs. Sanchez a folder. "Class, this is Roman Rodriguez, he's joining us for a while."

"Hey, Roman," a boy with wild dark hair in the back row called out, "You're my *primo*." I scrunched my face up. "Your cousin, man," he said to clarify. Then he stood up and shook his fist at the rest of the class, "And don't you guys try anything stupid with him because my dad told me that his dad is a war hero."

Everybody was staring at me now, but it actually didn't feel bad this time. Frankie, my cousin, seemed like he was a little bit older than the other students and was definitely a leader. Mrs. Sanchez told the kids to quiet down, and led me to a desk one row away from Frankie. She cautioned him, "Don't talk to your *primo* too much, Frankie. I don't want you to get him in trouble."

"Thanks, Frankie," I whispered, genuinely happy.

"No problem," he whispered back, "just wait till recess. I'll show you the ropes." He winked and had a kind of a crooked grin that was full of big, white teeth. I liked my *primo* already.

The funny thing was, I started to feel that El Puerto was more like home than my real house in Virginia. I was glad, but afraid, too. This seemed too good to be true. My mom and Bea were safe. Mrs. Martinez said she would pray for my dad, like Grandma did every day. I already had a new pet, and Coyote loved the *rancho*. Deep inside, I was expecting the worst. I just didn't know when it would happen.

At recess Frankie introduced me to his friends: Horace, Fidel, Jacob and Leon. The girls played by themselves and only came over by our tree to bug us when they wanted us to chase them. The boys wanted me to tell them about my dad since Frankie had bragged about him being a war hero.

"Does he have a lot of ribbons?" Horace asked.

"Does he carry a gun?" Leon wanted to know. The rest of the guys made fun of him for that one. "Sorry," said Leon, his feelings hurt, "Just wanted to know."

"Yeah, he is a pilot," I said, "So he actually carries a pistol, and his plane has big guns."

"Whoa. Cool. Have you ever fired it?" They were curious.

"Nah." I just shook my head and smiled. "He doesn't usually bring it home." I didn't tell them that my mom would kill me if I even thought about touching a gun when my dad wasn't with me.

"Hey, when is your dad coming to El Puerto?" I must have started to look sad or something because Frankie changed the subject. I was glad; I didn't like talking about Dad too much, especially Dad and the war and when he might come back.

The guys started a game of touch football and included me. "You wanna be quarterback today?" Nice guys, I thought, and then I surprised them with my best spiral pass.

Close to the end of recess, Frankie grabbed my arm and pointed out one of the girls playing jacks on the edge of the basketball court, "Hey, Pauline likes you." I looked up and saw her watching me. A dark haired girl wearing a pink jacket. She waved, then giggled with the rest of the girls and ran back to the building.

Frankie's older sister, from the high school, picked us up on her way home. "Mom told me to take you home every day. I'm your cousin, Marlene." She drove fast down the main road then turned onto the dirt road toward the ranch.

"So even if the little twirp isn't at school," she motioned to Frankie. "Wait for me on the corner like today." She dropped me off at Grandpa's mailbox.

Coyote ran to meet me, and I raced him to the house. I flung the door open.

"How was school today, Roman?" Grandma asked, just setting a plateful of *bizcochitos* and a cold glass of milk on the table for me.

"Great!" I grabbed two cookies, washed them down with the milk and was out the door to find Beans.

School continued pretty good. After all, I was just staying a couple of months. Nothing bad had happened yet. I liked my cousin Frankie, and Mrs. Sanchez was nice. She brought us food every Friday for afternoon snacks. Mrs. Sanchez made all the wedding cakes for El Puerto, so we got a lot of her trial run cakes and cookies.

Mom had been making regular phone calls from Germany, and I talked to her every time she called. Dad was stable. He was still in a coma, but the doctors said that was the best thing for him right now. His leg was healing. They expected him to wake up any day now. Bea was learning a few words in German, and the Air Force base had a pre-school where she could go; my mom helped out there when she could.

The phone calls were mostly always the same; she'd talk to Grandma then me. How was school? Do you have friends? Are you being good to Grandma? Are you helping with your chores? I'd fill her in on my life while Grandma and Grandpa went to the living room and whispered about what Mom had told Grandma.

Then everything just stopped, and my life changed in one day.

10

Trouble

I remember the call came early on Ash Wednesday. Grandma and I were eating breakfast and Grandpa Joe was ready to take me to school since it was snowing a little. Grandma answered in her usual cheery voice, *"Buenos Dias,"* then immediately said to Grandpa, "Joe, get on the other line, hurry."

After lots of "uh huhs and don't worry Cindy, we will be praying for him," they both hung up. "What's going on?" I asked. I knew it was bad.

"Nothing, *mi hito*," Grandma said. She was wiping her eyes with her apron.

"That's not true, Grandma. Tell me what's happening to my dad. What did Mom tell you?" I wanted answers. At that moment, I realized that they had been hiding the truth from me for a while—all three of them. They thought I was too young and too weak to know the truth.

Grandpa walked in from the other room, blowing his nose. He sat at his regular place at the table, stunned. "Grandpa, what's wrong?" One glance at Grandma told him he shouldn't say anything, but one glance at me broke his will to keep the secret.

"Is my dad dead?" I asked, so he wouldn't have to say it.

He grabbed me in a bear hug, "No, no Roman. He's not dead, not even close. Sit down and I'll tell you. Then you have to promise to go to school. Your mom and dad want you to have as normal a life as possible, and that means going to school today, even if we get there a little bit late."

He explained how Dad had woken up, come out of his coma and even talked with Mom and Bea. Then, all of a sudden, he tried to move and couldn't feel his legs. The doctors thought it was just the pain medication, but they tested his legs by poking sharp pins in him from his feet to his thighs. Everything below his waist was lifeless.

I knew what that meant. I'd seen Ida Green's dad in a wheelchair. She had to push him around the base until he got discharged. He couldn't be in the military any more. Ida was scared. She'd grown up as a military kid and didn't know what civilian life would be like. Her mom had to go to work to bring in money for their family. "Will he have to be in a wheelchair?"

Grandma started crying again and left the room. "Maybe," Grandpa said. "But it's early. The best thing is that your dad can talk with us next time they call. He wants to hear from you Roman. He needs to talk with his son." Grandpa's voice broke just a little.

"Now finish your milk, and I'll get the truck warmed up." He whispered in my ear. "Go find your grandma and give her a hug. Men comfort women when trouble comes, Roman."

I looked for Grandma around the house, opening doors quietly and shutting them. Then I opened the door to a room where I never went—Grandma called it *La Capilla*, her little chapel. It smelled good in there, like candle wax and incense from church. She was kneeling in front of a small statue of St. Anthony.

I liked St. Anthony—his name was my middle name. I was always asking him to help me find lost stuff, just like the nuns at my old school taught me. "Tony, Tony turn around; what is lost will now be found." Maybe he could help with my dad.

She put her hand out to me. "Roman, come here and help me pray for your dad." I knelt down beside her, put my arm around her waist and rested my head against her shoulder. I listened to her repeat the prayers as she moved the rosary through her fingers. "Now you say a special prayer to ask the Blessed Mother and St. Anthony to help your father." She waited a couple of minutes. "Okay?" she asked. I nodded. "You must go to school now. I'm sure Grandpa is waiting."

"But I..." I protested. School would be very hard for me today. "Can't I just stay home and play with Beans?"

"No, your dad wouldn't want you to," she said quietly, a faraway smile playing around her lips. "I'll stay here and pray today; you go to school. We all have our jobs, Roman. Besides, today is Ash Wednesday. I need to get some special cooking done for tonight after Mass."

School wasn't so bad. The kids just kept asking me what was wrong and why I didn't want to play until Frankie told them to leave me alone. "It's alright, *Primo*," he commiserated. "When my dad left to work in Albuquerque for a while, I used to get sad too. He wouldn't come home for weeks. At least he could call us..." his voice trailed off.

I turned the last smile I had in my face to him, "Thanks, Frankie. They said that he might call tomorrow." Then I sat by the wall, alone, just waiting for lunch to end.

11

The Stations

I never really liked church. Oh yeah, I had done everything the nuns wanted, all my catechism and stuff at school. But I got bored in church. Sing, talk, sing, talk, shake hands, talk, talk, talk. Well, the shaking hands was fun. I had a special, demented hand shake I used to make old ladies feel sorry for me, but I got whapped in the head by my mom when she caught me.

Tonight we were going to Mass at San Antonio. People around El Puerto said the name of the church so fast that I didn't realize until later that the old adobe church was dedicated to St. Anthony. There was a big statue of him in the back and lots of candles were lit for the prayers people needed help with.

Grandma lit one candle a week for our family since she had gotten married and moved to El Puerto, which was over fifty years ago. Now, she and I would light another, a special one for my dad. I prayed that he would get better and be able to use his legs again. I cried just a little thinking about how he might never be able to play football with me or show me how to pitch.

Mass started, and Father Ortega droned on. The singing was sure different here. It sounded like a fiesta not a Mass, but I liked the music. Then we got our ashes. "Remember that you are dust and to dust you will return," is what the priest told us. I didn't think they should say that to everybody—maybe Grandma and Grandpa should hear it, but I didn't want to think about that.

Now everybody had a big black cross on their foreheads to remind us that we were all going to die anyway. How depressing, I thought. I zoned out until the end of Mass, thinking about my mom, Bea and Dad and looking around at the inside of the church.

The Stations of the Cross at my old church in Virginia were boring. They were just plain wooden crosses with gold Roman numerals at the bottom. During Lent, the whole school would go over to listen to the Stations once a week. Of course, only the good kids got to read, so I just sat with my class and got bored. I usually got moved twice for talking or fidgeting before we filed out and back to class.

San Antonio, our church at El Puerto, was different. The stations were painted on flat pieces of wood and outlined with a dark purple stripe all the way around. And these paintings were big—if you stared at them long enough, you could pretend you were really there.

We were sitting by the fifth station, where Simon helps Jesus carry the cross. I liked that one—the way Simon smiled at Jesus, you could tell he was glad to help, but his eyes were sad, and he looked kind of scared about the whole thing. It's hard getting pulled in to something that is so dangerous, especially when you're not sure what to do.

But at least he was doing something to help. Me? All I did was run around with Beans and Frankie while my mom was at the hospital every day, and my dad was hooked up to tubes and couldn't even walk.

I guess I'd been staring at the picture for a long time because Grandma tapped me on the head and pointed toward the front of the church as Father Ortega gave the final blessing.

We filed out in silence. Church was supposed to make you feel better, not worse. I guess the only thing I could look forward to now was Grandma's special meal. Maybe she made cookies again. I could use one, but I didn't hold out much hope.

Dad told me that Grandma and Grandpa gave up eating meat on Wednesdays and Fridays during the forty days of Lent. When he was my age, she made him do extra chores and put spare pennies in an old sock to be given to the poor on Good Friday.

"They were pretty strict about all that stuff, Ro," he told me. "But, I'll tell you, it sure helped me later on. If I could get through Lent with Grandma and Grandpa, I figured I could get through anything, even flight school," he joked. I hoped it wouldn't be too hard.

When we got home, Grandma set a meager meal of beans spiced with chili, homemade tortillas and no dessert. "It's the beginning of Lent, Roman. Time for us to sacrifice. We won't eat anything sweet for forty days. Then when Easter comes, it will be so good. We will have pie, cookies, pudding, anything you want!"

"Okay," my voice listless and uninspired. I ate only because I was hungry. "Can I go play with Beans now?"

As I left the room, I heard Grandpa Joe tell Grandma, "I'm going to take him this year. He can do it, Maria."

"I don't know, Joe. He's so little. What if something happened to you?" She started to cry, and Grandpa comforted her.

"*Ay mujer*, don't worry. God will provide for us and our family as He has always done. Junior is going to be fine, I know it." Then I could hear his voice change and get stronger, "But I want to make the walk not just for Junior. Roman needs this too."

"We'll see," she said.

12

Bueno

The next day, Grandpa was rummaging through the barn when I went out to go to school.

"Are you ready, Grandpa?" When I saw that the keys were on the hood of the truck, I asked, "Do you want me to warm her up?" He'd been letting me get the feel of the truck for a few days. I'd start the truck with the clutch in, let it run a minute or so, then put it in neutral and pull the brake until we were ready to go.

"Sure, Roman, get 'er going. I'm looking for my bicycle. I've got to start training."

"Training? For what?"

"The walk, Roman. We've only got thirty-eight days until we make the walk for your father. And I am going to be in shape."

I looked puzzled. I guess I had heard right in the kitchen last night. We were going for a walk, but Grandpa was old. How far could he go, I wondered. How far did we need to go? And why would we be walking for my dad?

He pulled an old time bike out from behind a stack of roofing tin. Smiling, he showed it to me as he dusted it off with a red bandanna. "Pretty *suave*, huh, Roman?"

"Yeah, Grandpa, I guess so." I lied. It was the ugliest

bike I'd ever seen. An old five speed with an ugly plastic seat and butterfly handlebars. It had been spray painted cherry red. You could see where the original pin striping must have been by the raised lines of red paint on the fenders. He put it in the yard then we both jumped in the warm truck.

"How are *you* gonna train, Roman?"

"What do you mean, Grandpa Joe?"

"I mean, what are you going to do to get ready?"

"I don't even know what you're talking about," I said, exasperated. "How hard can it be to go for a walk? I do it all the time when Frankie's sister drops me off at the mailbox. And I really don't think you could probably go any farther than that." I'd finally had enough; sometimes the people around El Puerto, including my grandparents assumed I knew everything about this place. Sure, Dad talked a lot about El Puerto, when he was home, but I never really bothered to listen—walking to school in the snow, five miles each way. I just figured it was part of what parents said to make their kids obey the rules and think that they had it easy.

"Whoa," said Grandpa, and he stopped the truck in the driveway. I thought he was going to be mad at me. Instead, he said, "Yeah, that's right, you don't listen so good do you? 'Cause I know your dad talked to you about this. But I'll tell you again." I couldn't tell if he was being serious or sarcastic, so I decided to hear his story.

"And don't worry if I make you late for school," he winked, and I settled down to listen.

"You know that our ancestors came here to this valley over four hundred years ago. El Puerto was one of the first villages to be settled by the Spaniards. We mixed with the local people. They showed us a lot of good stuff, like how to raise corn and chile. We showed them how to irrigate with the ditches and make the land productive with sheep and cattle. We also traded some ideas about our religions."

I interrupted, "Sr. Anne, my catechism teacher in Virginia, said that the Indians were pagans. I didn't think we were supposed to trade ideas with them—especially about religion."

"Well," Grandpa continued, "Maybe back in Virginia that's the case. But here in New Mexico, we learned to live with each other. In fact, way back, my great-great Grandfather Eusebio Martinez was married to a pueblo woman from Santa Clara, just up the road. That blood runs through our veins today."

Wow, I thought, wait till I tell Adam in Virginia. He thought he was so cool because his dad had an arrowhead collection. My ancestors made the arrowheads!

"Are you bored yet, Roman? Ready to go to school?" I knew Grandpa was joking. He could see the expression on my face; I was ready to hear more.

"No way," I yelled. "And Grandpa, it's not just because I'm missing school. This stuff is neat, and we're a part of it."

"*Bueno*," he said and shook his head approvingly. "Then that is the right reason to continue." He turned off the truck engine; we sat together in the warmth of the cab.

"Roman, I want you to know that this land is sacred. Not just because we know God has given it to us to care for and look after," he looked out of the windshield as if he was seeing something faraway. "This land is holy. The native people knew that, and our Spanish ancestors knew it, too. When the troubles came between our people, it was too dangerous to send the missionary priests here, so the men of our community got together to worship. They led the songs, the prayers, and the pilgrimages."

Grandpa paused then looked at me as if he were delivering a quiet but powerful secret. "These men were your ancestors. They are leaders, like your own father, Roman. And this walk, the pilgrimage, is the first step in your journey to join these good men who have been the leaders of your family."

I didn't know what to say. There was a good silence between us. Had Grandpa given the same talk to Dad when he was a boy? I finally managed to ask, "Where do we walk to, Grandpa?"

"Well, about two hundred years ago, a man was out tending his fields, only about a dozen miles away from here, when he found a cross stuck in the ground. He wondered who had put it there and because he felt it was holy, he took it to the church at Santa Cruz.

"The next morning, when he went out to plow again, the same cross was there in the same place. This time, that man fell to his knees, praising God, and he vowed to build a church right on that spot. That is where we will walk."

"You mean the church is still there, with the cross that he found?"

"Sure, Roman, the people of the villages have cared for the cross and the church for the last two centuries. It is our responsibility to God and to our ancestors. When we have a special favor to ask of God, like we do this year, we walk. We are pilgrims," he looked at me and smiled thoughtfully, "*peregrinos* in Spanish. We wander in search of an answer."

"An answer to my prayer that Dad gets better?"

"Yes," he sighed. Then took a look at his watch. "We'd better get you to school, young man. Mrs. Sanchez will be very mad at me if you miss the whole morning." He revved up the engine.

We were both quiet on the way to school. Me, thinking about all he had told me; Grandpa thinking about the past. I gathered my backpack and lunch, shut the door and was halfway to the school yard gate when I remembered something. I ran back to the truck and motioned for Grandpa to roll down his window.

"Thanks, Grandpa. Thanks for telling me about who we are."

We gave each other our special handshake. "See you tonight, *hito*."

I ran up the stairs to class, happy to know I could finally do something to help my dad.

13

Spring Training

We were in training. Like a couple of boxers getting ready for a big fight, Grandpa and I started our forty days preparing for the pilgrimage walk. Every morning, I'd watch him pedaling up and down the lane to the *rancho* before breakfast. I could look out my window and watch him on that old bicycle he'd found in the barn. Five times up, five times back, and that was before he even had a cup of coffee.

I dedicated myself to running. I figured that would keep up my stamina. I had never walked ten miles before, so I was kind of scared about pooping out before we reached the church. I ran everywhere, but especially up and down the stairs; in fact, I ran up and down any stairs I could find. I apologized everyday to Grandma for clumping up and down the stairs to my bedroom, and she forgave the noise because she knew that Grandpa and I were going to represent our family on the walk.

After school, I told Marlene to drop me off just a little farther away from the house each day. Then I'd run all the way home. "Geez, Roman, what are you trying to do," she asked one day, curious about my routine. "You gonna run a marathon or something?"

"Getting ready for the pilgrimage," I said. Since she'd been raised in El Puerto, she knew.

Her eyes got big, and she looked concerned. "Where's Grandpa Joe starting from this year?"

"Grandma said the church at Nambé, but I'm not really sure. Why?" I asked, ready to bolt out of the truck to start my run.

"Just watch out for him... he's crazy on that walk. You don't know how far ten miles is until you walk it with Grandpa Joe."

"Why, have you done the walk before, Marlene?"

"Me?" she questioned then waved her hand like she was swishing flies, "No way. Too tough, but my brother went with him one year. The blisters on his feet didn't heal for a month! Anyway, aren't you kind of little to go?"

"Not if I train, Marlene. Don't worry, I'll be alright. We're walking for my dad, so I've got to do it this year."

"Okay, Romeo," she sometimes called me that when she wanted to act like my big sister. "I'll light a candle for you on the morning of the walk. Wait, no," she laughed, "not one candle, it'll have to be two, one for each foot!" She laughed again and put the truck in gear waiting till I slammed the door and started running up the road before she peeled out.

One thing about a pilgrimage, it's not just about whether you can walk ten miles. Grandma taught me how to prepare another way. Each night, after I finished my homework, we would go into her *capilla* and say one decade of the rosary. Her routine was always the same. She'd go in to stoke up the corner fireplace then light a candle in front of the Virgin of Guadalupe. She had a picture of my dad in his uniform and then a family picture, with all of us together, on the altar that Grandpa had made her.

It was dark, except for the light from the fire and candle. Sometimes it was so peaceful there, that I couldn't stay awake through even one decade of the rosary. Grandpa would come in and walk me, half asleep, up the stairs to my room.

"Don't worry, Roman," Grandma would tell me in the morning, as I'd eat my breakfast, "your guardian angel finished the prayers for you."

14

Pilgrimage

The big day was coming. It seemed a little weird looking forward to Good Friday, since that is supposed to be a day when we remember Christ's suffering. It's also a day when you can't eat meat, sweets, and have to sit in church for three hours straight, unless you are going on the pilgrimage. Then you get to walk! You are still thinking about Jesus, but in a really different way. It's more like you don't just think about the Way of the Cross, you actually do it!

My grandparents seemed to be in church a lot during Lent, I guess for a couple of reasons. Grandma said it was the holiest time of the year, plus she was always praying to ask the Virgin of Guadalupe to help my dad. I knew that she was praying all the time for our family, and her eyes were starting to get dark circles underneath. In a way, I think she went on her own pilgrimage that year. She and Mary; they were both moms who had sons that were suffering. We were all asking God the same question—will You please help my dad get well and bring our family back together?

I'd never really thought of my dad as somebody's son before. It was good to remember that he had grown up with Grandma and Grandpa Joe. I knew that he left because he wanted adventure, but Grandma said that he would come back to El Puerto because this was where his heart and soul wanted to be.

It was almost Easter Sunday. On Thursday night after Mass, Grandma started baking her special *bizcochitos*. The whole house smelled of cinnamon and anise. She whispered to me that even though it was Good Friday tomorrow, she would give Grandpa Joe a bag of them for the walk. It was so cozy in the warm kitchen. The moon was nearly full, and the light shone in the windows. Grandma's stove glowed a warm and fiery yellow every time I stuck a piece of wood in to keep up the temperature. You could see the gold through the cracks on the stove's black top.

Since we weren't allowed to watch TV or listen to music, it gave me time to think. Could I be happy here always? Not like my dad who wanted to fly, but like Grandpa who stayed with his family.

"You can't go on vacation when you have goats and chickens," Grandpa had warned me early on when I said that I wanted to go see a movie in Santa Fe. "But living here is worth the sacrifice, Roman." Now I was starting to understand why. Grandpa Joe wasn't just in love with Grandma and his family; he also loved the land in a way that I really never knew about before. "You have to love it, in order to live on it," he said when I asked one day why Dad left El Puerto.

"Maybe Dad didn't love this place enough to stay?" I asked.

He answered me with fire in his eyes, "If you hate the work and don't see God in it, you will leave." Then he added quickly, "But people come back to the land and back to their families—and," he grabbed my shoulders and looked directly at me, "and they are always welcomed home, Roman. They are like lost sheep, returning to the flock."

Now, it was the night before the pilgrimage, and I couldn't imagine being anywhere else except right here in this warm kitchen with my grandparents. Grandpa Joe came in with a big forest service map and spread it out on the table. "You've been asking about the route for the last forty days, Roman. Now, I'm finally going to show you," he said. "We need to know where to start our walk tomorrow."

"Joe," warned Grandma, "I still think he's too young."

"And I'm too old!" laughed Grandpa Joe. "Maria, I walked this for my brother when I was his age," he pointed at me. "And now, we will walk it together...for his father." Grandpa Joe's voice got shaky. He quickly sipped his coffee.

Grandma smiled, came over and gave him a kiss on his forehead. She knew that this was an adventure for Grandpa, too. "*Ay*, my boys!" she said with mock exasperation.

When 8:30 came around, it was already dark. Grandpa Joe yawned and stretched. "Time for bed, Grandson. We have to get up early tomorrow." I got ready, kissed them both good night then settled into bed with a letter that my mom had just sent. She had been sending more letters because a lot of times it was hard for my dad to talk to us over the phone. He still couldn't hear so great because of the explosion, and he got frustrated when he couldn't understand what we were saying.

The last letter mom wrote actually had Dad's "chicken scratch" at the end. He wrote the last part just to me:

Dear Ro:
Don't let the old man make you work too hard. Be good

to G and G. Kiss them for me, Son.
I'll be home soon. I miss you.
Love,
Dad

The "old man" of course was Grandpa. I could tell that Grandpa probably made him do a lot of stuff around the *rancho*; maybe that was the reason he left for school and the Air Force. But I also knew that he loved them. It took a lot of effort for him to write; he wanted us all to know how he felt. I would carry that letter with me tomorrow. I needed something that he had held in his own hands to go with us on the journey.

15

The Best Friday

It was still dark outside when I heard Grandpa Joe walk upstairs. I had already woken up and looked at the blue numbers on the alarm clock—5:30—nearly time to go. I was up and had my t-shirt and jeans on when Grandpa walked in with his red suspenders still unfastened.

"Good morning." He was carrying something behind him. "Here, put this on." He offered a kid sized flight jacket with my dad's name on it: Junior. "It was your dad's when he was a little boy. It'll keep you warm. Come down for breakfast," he looked back. "You'll need a good cup of coffee in you today, *hito*." He smiled.

I tried the coat on, and it fit perfectly. I loved the feel of the leather coat. It was lined with real sheepskin and had a fur collar that was made of yellow wool. I guess dad had always dreamed about flying. I ran downstairs to show it off.

Grandma was cooking a special breakfast for us today. When she saw me, her eyes got red. "What's the matter, Grandma?"

She reached down and combed her fingers through my tussled hair. "Nothing is wrong," she sniffed. "It's just that you look so much like your father in that jacket." Then she chuckled, remembering, "Oh, I could not get him to take that thing off for at least a year. Even in the summer, he would wear it to go feed the goats and tend the chickens. He'd zoom around my kitchen like an airplane. Always telling me he was going to take off someday and fly so far above El Puerto that we'd only be able to hear his jet but not see it." She turned back to the stove, to stir a boiling pot.

I reached into a pocket and found a toy jet airplane. This one was really great—all metal and old. The tiny jet was still in my hand when Grandpa came in the kitchen for his last cup of coffee.

"Oh," he smiled, "I haven't seen that in a while." He picked up the jet. "It's a fighter plane, a very early version of what your dad's unit flies now." Grandpa whispered the last part because he didn't want to see Grandma cry anymore. He turned it over in his hand. "Roman, this plane has a peregrine engine; it's very fast," Grandpa stirred the sugar into his coffee.

"What's a peregrine, Grandpa," I said, my mouth full. "A bird?"

"Yes—a fast one, a falcon. It's like a little hawk. Your dad loved that bird. When he went to the Academy in Colorado, that was their mascot. The falcons."

"Do they live here, Grandpa? Can we see one?" I interrupted. I had a strange desire to see a peregrine now that I knew Dad liked them. The bird and the little plane reminded me about why we were always apart, always waiting for dad to come home. I looked at Grandma and thought, these two things were the reasons she cried.

"They live in cliffs, far up in the caves. They build their nests there in the spring and swoop down on the little critters in the fields to feed their babies. I don't know if it's too cold yet for them, but Easter is later this year, so maybe..."

Breakfast did not take any longer than our falcon conversation. We ate Grandma's fresh tortillas and the blue corn mush, *atole*, with cinnamon and sugar that was traditional on Good Friday. There would be no meat until Easter Sunday, the big feast day, when all my aunts, uncles and cousins would come to visit. For me, it was the first big holiday without my mom and my sister. I'd miss them.

16

Pilgrims

When we stopped at the Nambé church only about ten cars were already parked there. Grandpa got two sticks out of the back of the truck. "These are our walking sticks for the journey, Roman. This one is your size," he handed me a shorter version of his own.

Grandma stood in front of me with a kind of necklace made out of two small brown squares of cloth attached by ribbons. I had seen kids wear them under their shirts at the school in El Puerto. "This was your father's scapular," she said, "I want you to wear it today in honor of him and so Our Lady will protect you on the journey." She kissed it then put it around my neck. "Keep it safe, Roman."

I tucked it quickly inside my shirt. Then Grandpa Joe put on his backpack with the cheese and chile sandwiches, water bottles and cookies inside. We were ready!

"I'll meet you there," said Grandma. "You be careful with him, Joe." She looked at Grandpa Joe as she gave me a final hug and blessing. She did the same with Grandpa, "God bless you. Walk with God today." Then she did a strange thing; she took a picture of my dad out of her purse and gave it to Grandpa. "Walk for him; ask God to bring him home to us, Joe." She turned, so we couldn't see her cry.

Grandma climbed slowly into the truck and without waving goodbye headed back home to begin cooking for Sunday. Later she would wait for us to arrive at *El Santuario*, the end of our journey, and drive us back home.

"Don't worry about her, Roman; she just gets sentimental when she thinks about your dad," Grandpa said. "Let's get going before it gets too late."

We hit the road and found an easy rhythm with our sticks—step, step, scrunch as the tip of our walking sticks hit the gravelly shoulder of the road. I started thinking, ten miles... I was a little afraid because after we left the Nambé church and village, we didn't see many houses, just a long road, a few pilgrims and wide open spaces filled with hills, pinon trees and scrubby grasses.

After about a half hour, I asked "How far have we gone, Grandpa?"

He smiled, "Not so far yet, Roman. We'll go a little farther before we take a water break."

I was quiet and walked along the side of the highway, behind Grandpa Joe. I tried to match his pace. I liked the way his walking stick measured out the distance—tap and scrunch, tap and scrunch. A walk is a good place to think by yourself. I'd overheard Grandpa talking to Grandma about fulfilling his promise to God. I thought that walking for someone or something really could show that you loved them. Grandpa said that he had walked for his brother. What did his brother need so badly that Grandpa had to make the pilgrimage? Sixty years ago, I thought. That was a long, long time ago.

Time passed and soon I saw other pilgrims. Some walked carrying their backpacks. Like Grandpa, their bags were filled with the essentials to keep them going on the long journey—lots of water, granola bars, oranges. Some pilgrims ran. Even on this cold morning, they were dressed in shorts and t-shirts, their headphones in their ears and water bottles in their hands.

We had arrived early at the church, and there were only a few cars in the parking lot, so I couldn't figure out how there were so many pilgrims on the road now. I caught up with Grandpa Joe and asked.

"Well, different people start from different places. Some started out last night and walked all the way from Santa Fe; some walk two miles to the church, some walk seven or eight, and some can only make it from the *Santuario* parking lot. We all come from different places and head to the same spot on this day."

"Gee, that doesn't seem fair. Will their prayers be answered, too?"

He laughed, then grew serious, "Roman, it's not how far you walk, it's what is in your heart when you are walking."

"I know," I tried to convince him, "but we're walking ten miles. God knows we're sacrificing more than those who are just walking a few steps to the end."

"Yes, you may be right," he looked slyly, then pointed, "but do you see that man there?" He pointed out a pilgrim with a cactus wood cross attached to his backpack. I nodded. "Every year, he comes from Albuquerque; he starts his walk on Tuesday morning, and he finishes the hundred and twenty miles on Friday."

I couldn't say anything to that except, "Wow. A hundred twenty miles." Our conversation trailed off as we approached another group. These were ladies reciting the rosary as they walked. They all wore blue in honor of Mary. Grandpa knew some of them from El Puerto and smaller villages. He smiled slightly before saying, *"Buenos Dias le de Dios."* While they didn't interrupt their prayers, they did smile back.

I was proud of Grandpa Joe. He was the oldest walker we had seen so far, and I was the youngest. We were like book ends—and he was right, although we wouldn't be the pilgrims who had walked the farthest, we would be walking ten miles, and that's an accomplishment for anybody!

I won't say that the pilgrimage route was boring because at our pace, we kept catching up with all sorts of people. We walked past one lady who wore a red jogging suit, white tennis shoes and her little dog was prancing in front of her on a rhinestone leash and collar.

"That little dog will be tired before they reach the church," Grandpa said in a whisper to me, so he didn't offend the lady. I laughed. "Yeah," I whispered back, "that Chihuahua dog is so small, he has to take about ten steps for every one step the lady takes." Later on, when we saw her again, the little dog was riding in a front pack, just like a baby.

The road to *El Santuario* curves many times before you finish the ten miles. Sometimes you can see the people you passed on the bend in the road behind you. Sometimes you stop and rest to get a drink and other people catch up to you. Grandpa Joe told me, "It's like our lives, Roman. People come and go—but the people like you and me, we are paired for life because we are family. God is like that, too." Grandpa slowed down just a little, so he could talk to me. "He is walking with us, taking care of us." Then he stopped to look off in the distance and said, "And He is walking with your mom and dad and Bea, too, so they will come back to us... soon."

Just then, I got real scared for two reasons. The first reason was because Grandpa had hesitated too long to say "soon". I wondered many times during my stay in El Puerto if Dad would ever be well enough to come home. What if he never got better? What if he couldn't learn to walk or talk again? I had too many questions that I couldn't ask either Grandma or Grandpa. I touched my chest where the scapular was. Maybe Grandma was right; I just had to pray and walking made that easier.

I don't mean that I prayed like saying Our Father's and Glory Be's or anything. I just talked to God and let pictures of my family circle around in my head. I remembered the last time I saw Dad. I was so mad that he was leaving; I moped around for two days before we all went to the base for his deployment ceremony. The last thing he told me before he kissed Mom goodbye was, "Roman, be strong. Take care of your mother and sister while I'm away. I'm counting on you." I felt bad that I hadn't done a very good job of that in the past few months, and I thought about whether I'd get a second chance to do better.

The second thing that scared me was when we turned a corner in the road. I looked up and suddenly saw there was a man carrying a cross as big as himself, as big as the one above the altar in our parish church. I stopped and made a noise, like when a goat is scared, and it blows out its breath. Grandpa put his hand on my shoulder, "Nothing to be afraid of," he said quietly in my ear, and I got the idea that I should not stare at this strange pilgrim. When we passed him, though, I couldn't help it. I saw that he didn't have shoes on. He was walking barefoot the whole way. His shirt was off, and he was only wearing jean cutoffs. His left arm had a cross tattooed on it, and his right shoulder was already bleeding a little from the weight of the cross.

He sang the saddest song that I'd ever heard. It was beautiful in a way, but his voice sounded like he wanted to cry. I picked up the melody real fast, and Grandpa and I hummed along with him as the song's sad rhythm matched the speed of our walking. On the cross, he had a picture of a soldier from a long ago war. He was wearing green combat clothes and an army helmet. He carried a rifle but was smiling for the camera.

The man with the cross wore a look of pained concentration, and you could tell that each step hurt even though he walked on the black top of the road. We heard his mournful song on the wind for a long time after we passed him.

17

Questions

I looked at Grandpa. He knew I had so many questions to ask. I wondered how far this man had come and how long it had taken him. Grandpa checked his watch. "We've been on the road for a while, Roman. Should we take a break?"

I wanted to rest, but I was afraid to see the barefooted man again. He made me feel so sad inside. We would have to pass him again on the way to *El Santuario* if we stopped now. "Is it allowed?" I asked. "Will God be mad at us for resting?"

"Sure, it's okay," Grandpa smiled big. "I know a place right over there under some big trees. God wants us to finish our pilgrimage, and so we must rest a little bit." He chuckled, "And Grandma's heart would be broken if we didn't eat her sandwiches."

As we sat down in the shade of a small cottonwood, it felt good to get some water and food. The sky was so blue with a few cotton puff clouds circling the high green mountains to the northeast. The sage brush smelled good, like the way Beans smelled when she had been outside all night, cool and crisp. Grandpa drank out of the canteen on his belt then offered it to me. The water tasted like metal from the aluminum canteen, but it was cold and washed down the cheese and chile sandwiches Grandma put in his pack.

"You want this half?" he asked. "Sure," I grabbed it and wolfed it down. "And don't forget that Grandma put cookies in there for us, too," I hinted, still hungry and wanting some sugar.

When we were almost done, Grandpa Joe cleared the ground of rocks and small twigs in front of us. Then he began to draw in the sandy soil. It looked like this:

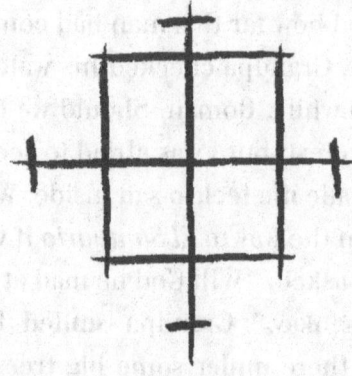

"Grandson," he began very seriously. "I know that you have many questions." I nodded. "But this is the answer to all of them."

"Is it a maze?" I wondered aloud. "A puzzle?"

"Very good, Roman," he nodded approving my guess.

"Grandpa," I said quietly, thinking. "You and Grandma keep telling me that we are walking for Dad. But she gets so sad every time we talk about him. I'm scared that he's never coming home."

Grandpa reached over to give me a hug. "It's okay to be scared. In fact, when I was your age, I walked this same route for my brother who was away at the war." Grandpa lowered his voice and said quietly, "He didn't come home."

"Did you get mad at God?" I asked as he wiped his eyes.

"Yes, many times, especially during the year we found out he was killed. It was really hard on my mother. I could understand the death of a soldier, but I couldn't understand how God could cause something to happen that would hurt my mother so much."

"Was she like Grandma?"

"Yes, very much," he agreed and winked. "Why do you think I married Grandma? She is very much like my mother—kind, caring, prayerful. It hurts me to see your Grandma worrying so much and feeling so bad. And you too, I know it hasn't been easy for you to come to a strange place, go to school with different kids, and not have your mom around. I'm not just walking for your dad, I'm walking for you, too.

"My grandfather took me with him for the same reasons sixty years ago," he continued. "We probably stopped at this same tree," he looked around, wondering. "What he showed me and told me worked. I stopped being so mad—about the war, about my brother, about everything, and especially about God."

"What did he tell you, Grandpa?"

Grandpa Joe looked down again at the drawing in the dirt. "My grandfather drew this for me, too. What do you think this means?"

"Well, it's like a cross, but it has too many arms and boxes." I stood up to see if it looked any different from another angle.

"Good guess, Roman. It is a cross, but it is also many crosses. It is a map, a path for our lives. You see everyone travels a path—far or near, but we all come back to the center."

"Here," I pointed.

"Yes, look at you. You have already begun your journey and come from so very far away to your home here in El Puerto. Today you are traveling back to the center."

"But what about your brother?" I questioned, not sure I wanted to know the answer. "He didn't return home, did he? He died in the war."

Grandpa Joe thought a minute about how to explain his answer. He looked at the hills and breathed in the clean morning air. "When I take this journey, my brother walks with me, as does my son," he smiled at me, "and my grandson."

I don't know if I really believed him, but I wanted to. "But what if Dad can't walk again?" I started to cry a little just thinking about it.

"We all do good for others, Roman. Look at your dad; he has been defending the country. I can't fly a plane and neither can you, so your dad has to do it for us. For all of us."

"Yeah, but why does it always have to be him?"

"I don't know, Roman. I wonder the same thing myself sometimes. I can only tell you what my grandfather told me. Your father is at a different point in his journey, and because he is not here with us, as the leaders of his family, we must walk for him.

"I guess we're all pilgrims, Roman," said Grandpa Joe. "All *peregrinos*."

"What does that mean?"

"A *peregrino* is a wanderer, a person who is always on a journey."

"Sounds like peregrine," I suggested, remembering breakfast.

"Yes, the peregrine falcons we talked about this morning," Grandpa smiled, but his brow was knit together like he was thinking. "They have a wide range, but come back to the cliffs they were born in to raise their chicks."

He got up and packed the backpack with the remains of our lunch and trash, but was still shaking his head at the coincidence of our conversation as we headed back to the road.

I felt better with lunch digesting and the knowledge that people in my family had made this journey many times before me.

The rest of the walk was mostly for thinking. Many hills fell behind us as new ones would take their place ahead. When the turn-off came for Chimayo, the village of *El Santuario*, I felt like I could keep going another ten miles. We stopped for a water break and gazed off into the distance. The blue hills of Taos about forty miles away were still topped with snow, and the Pajarito mesas of Los Alamos were beginning to glow green as we watched the rain clouds dump spring moisture twenty miles to the southwest.

"Not much further now, Roman." Grandpa said as we stuffed our water bottles back in the pack.

"What's *El Santuario* like?" I asked, trying to say the Spanish word with just the right accent. I'd been to the National Cathedral in Washington, DC. That was a big, big, church. I wasn't expecting anything like that, but I was kind of surprised when Grandpa Joe explained, "The church is very similar to ours in El Puerto, perhaps a third longer. But just mud adobes and vigas. You'll see soon enough." He bent down to zip up the bag and grabbed my hand, "I'm proud of you, Roman. I know your dad will be proud too when he hears about this."

Then peaceful silence accompanied us once again until we reached the village of Chimayo.

18

The Peregrine

We'd been walking about five hours when we headed up a steeper hill, and at the top looked down over the village of Chimayo. There were lots of cars there now. Many people, older than Grandpa who couldn't make the walk, came with their wheelchairs and walkers. Their families helped them to the gates of the churchyard.

As we walked down to the village, it was kind of quiet, especially considering the number of people standing around waiting in line to get into the church. I saw a few of the pilgrims who had passed us along the road. The barefoot man with the cross wasn't there yet, but the red suited lady was just getting out of a car with her dog when we arrived.

Grandpa chuckled, "Somebody must have felt sorry for the dog." I laughed too.

Pilgrims were spread out all over the village. Some lucky ones were already eating at the few cafés, and others were sticking their feet into the cool water of a little ditch that ran in front of the church. Good friends who hadn't seen each other all year met up again. In hushed tones, because it was nearly noon on Good Friday, people greeted each other.

"Joe," an older man in overalls and a straw hat tapped Grandpa on the shoulder. "Joe is that you?"

Grandpa Joe and his friend gave each other a big *abrazo*, patting each other on the back and shaking hands. "It's been too long, *compadre*," Grandpa Joe said. "Here, this is my grandson, Roman. Junior's boy. He made the walk this year with me all the way from Nambé." I liked the way he introduced me, like he was so proud of what we had accomplished.

"Roman, this is Ambrosio Valdez. He was the best man at my wedding."

"*Buenos Dias le de Dios*, Roman." Ambrosio gave me a greeting and blessing all in one and shook my hand. "Glad to know that you got this old man out of the house to get some exercise today." Both Grandpa Joe and Ambrosio seemed like they had lost forty years as they talked and joked around until Grandpa said, "Well, we better get in line. It's the first time the boy has been to the church. I want him to go in before it gets too late."

We said our goodbyes and stood in line for thirty minutes before we got close to the doors of the church. It was getting hot outside, but Grandpa had brought a couple of rosaries and told me to pray while we waited since it would pass the time.

Mostly I just moved the beads between my fingers. I tried to pray, but kept thinking about Mom and Dad and Bea. I didn't even know if I would hear from them for Easter.

Once we got inside the doors of the church, it was cool and dark. It was quiet but not silent, and we stood behind other pilgrims waiting to go into a little room off to the side. Grandpa was right, this place was old. As we inched our way along the main aisle, I saw lots of figures of the saints, not made out of plaster but carved over a hundred years ago out of cottonwood stumps. A lot of them were scary. Some of the statues had real wigs on and were dressed in silk with jewels. Some of them were bloody and showed the sufferings of Christ on the cross. I looked at these life size images and thought of my dad. Did he have to suffer like that? What about the men who had been in the bombing with him? How much pain had he been in and for how long?

I knew my mother had tried to keep up my spirits by not crying on the phone and writing only about the progress Dad was making, but I could see how hard it must be for her. A person doesn't ever really think of their dad with blood all over them, but that's what happened. As I stood in the church that day, I was determined that I would stand tall and be brave for my family. No more fighting, no more anger. I had to get over it. My mom, Bea, my dad, Grandma and Grandpa Joe, they were hurting too. If I could make this walk for Dad, I could learn to do other hard things, like forgetting the anger and helping out a lot more. I looked up at the altar and saw the image drawn there that Grandpa had sketched on the ground. It was the cross of the *peregrinos*, the pilgrims' cross.

I was there—in the center of the church, in the center of my family, in the center of the cross. Maybe someday, I'd be able to bring the rest of my family here to know the peace that Grandpa and I felt.

We walked into the little side room. In the floor was a hole about eighteen inches around. Inside something very simple, just dirt, but people believed it was miraculous. Grandpa and I scooped out a handful and put it in a plastic baggie, not too much since other people wanted some, too. As we exited the room to return to the church, he pointed out the photos of loved ones, crutches, leg braces, prayer cards all put up to show the healing that had occurred at this church.

He bent down and whispered in my ear. "This is the real miracle, Roman. The faith of the people. Whatever happens, this is always here for us." Then he took the photo of my dad that Grandma had given him and tacked it to a board that had pictures of men and women in uniform from many different wars.

I gave him a hug and said, "I know, Grandpa. I saw the pilgrims' cross." As I pointed it out, we both heard a murmuring in the crowd. Someone important was coming through the entrance of the church.

The darkness silhouetted the figure who was walking with a cane. "Perhaps it's the Archbishop," said Grandpa. "Maybe they are getting ready for Mass." The crowd parted for the man. As he got closer to the front, we noticed he was not wearing the robes of the church. He was wearing a hat, but not the Archbishop's tall mitre. Slowly, he limped up the main aisle, looking for something or someone. Clad in a blue uniform and a cap that shaded his eyes, he slowly made the sign of the cross in front of the altar, and as the light shone on his face, both Grandpa and I rushed forward.

We hugged, we cried, we laughed, we stood at arm's length and looked at each other. And then Dad told me in a halting and raspy voice, "I'm home, Roman. Home."

They could barely separate us when Mom and Bea came up the aisle with Grandma. Even the worshipers, so silent and reverent on this day, began to grin and smile. A few even clapped for us. Grandpa continued to say to anyone who would listen as we began to walk down the main aisle of the church and out into the sunshine, "My son is home; it is a miracle, a miracle!"

I just looked. I couldn't believe Dad was home. He put his hand on my shoulder as I helped him out of the church. I would be strong for him now. I took one glance backward and checked the pilgrim's cross painted high above the altar. Grandpa was right—at the center of everything, we all belonged.

Mom bent down to kiss me and hugged me way too long. But I let her. I had missed her too, more than I even realized. Bea tagged along behind us, wanting to hold my hand, and this time I picked her up and held her. It felt good to know I could be there for my family. I was not a kid anymore; I knew this myself. Grandpa's eyes filled with pride for me. My dad let me know that our family was going to be better than ever, and I would play a big role in making this work.

Grandma already had one of the picnic tables set for us out behind the church. Pots of beans and chile, homemade tortillas, *calabacitas* and Dad's favorite dessert, *natillas* made with fluffy egg whites, sugar and cinnamon, were ready.

"On the day of a miracle, you can eat sweets, even if it is Good Friday," said Grandma, this time through tears of joy. It was delicious!

Dad didn't talk very much; he still had some trouble speaking, but that was to be expected. He grinned though—a big wide grin that told us all how happy he was to be truly home.

Grandpa kept telling Mom, Grandma and Bea that they should appreciate the fact that he couldn't talk yet, because once he got started they wouldn't be able to shut him up. Everybody laughed, including Dad who shook his head. After lunch, while Mom and Grandma cleaned up, and Bea took a nap on blankets under the cottonwoods, Grandpa asked my dad and me to come with him, down to the little stream that ran behind the church.

"Bring your walking stick, Roman," he reminded me. Dad and I walked slowly down to where Grandpa was sitting on a river rock wall. It was calm and peaceful. A green alfalfa field lay beyond, and beyond that the high cliffs and caves made of red clay and sandstone. "Do you remember this, Son?" he asked Dad, tenderly.

"Yes," Dad replied halting between each word. "Good...memories...here." They both smiled, thinking about past pilgrimages made together. Stories shared and prayers answered. Grandpa pulled out a pocket knife. "Look, here," he pointed and showed me his walking stick. "Every walk taken is marked with a ring and the year."

"Kind of like a tree, huh, Grandpa?"

"Yes, it marks the history of our family—the prayers, the miracles, the journeys to home and family and this valley. So, Roman, how should we mark the journey of this year?"

He was asking me. This year's pilgrimage was so special it would require a special symbol. Perhaps something with three lines, maybe the pilgrim's cross. Then, we saw them. Two hunters, flying in the sky with a young one trailing behind.

Grandpa pointed, "Roman, look, your peregrines."

Sure enough, it was a pair of falcons with a fledgling. They were circling the field, looking, searching, gliding on the cool air currents of early spring. Without diving, they circled once more then headed home to their nests high in the rose colored cliffs. "They are going home, Roman."

It took tremendous effort for Dad to speak, "Home... to...stay." He smiled but his eyes were wet, and he put his arms around both Grandpa and me. So the three walking sticks, Grandpa's, mine and my dad's cane, were carved that day with three lines and the head of a falcon.

When Dad protested, "I...didn't...walk", I knew exactly what to say. "Yes, you did, Dad. There wasn't one step that I took without you."

19

Together

Mom, Grandma and Bea came down the hill. "Things are packed up," said Grandma, "and I don't want you tiring Junior. He still needs his rest."

Mom kissed me on the top of the head and said, "Help your father." It was what I would hear many times over the next few months. I smiled, thankful that I had a father to help.

In fact, we never moved back to Virginia. Dad was on medical leave for a year, and I finished school in El Puerto that year. Although it was crowded, last year was one of the best—living with Grandma and Grandpa, Mom and Dad, Bea and Beans. Oh, and don't forget Coyote!

Now, Dad has a job at Kirtland Air Force Base. I go to school in a bigger city, but we're only a couple of hours away from El Puerto, so we visit whenever we can. Grandpa will need help with the goats this summer, and Grandma will be teaching Bea how to bake *bizcochitos* when she grows up a little more.

www.ingramcontent.com/pod-product-compliance
Lightning Source LLC
Chambersburg PA
CBHW012151260626
47155CB00020B/3576